TH_
BASE

First published in Great Britain 1999 by Mammoth
an imprint of Egmont Children's Books Limited
239 Kensington High Street, London W8 6SA
Published in hardback by Heinemann Library,
a division of Reed Educational and Professional Publishing Limited
by arrangement with Egmont Children's Books Limited.
Text copyright © Carlo Gébler 1999
Illustrations copyright © Dan Williams 1999
The Author and Illustrator have asserted their moral rights.
Paperback ISBN 0 7497 3133 8
Hardback ISBN 0 431 06193 9
10 9 8 7 6 5 4 3 2 1
A CIP catalogue record for this title
is available from the British Library.
Printed at Oriental Press Limited, Dubai.

Carlo Gébler

THE BASE

Illustrated by Dan Williams

🍌 YELLOW BANANAS

For my godson,

Gabriel Hudson

C.G.

For my nephew,

Ramzi

D.W.

Chapter One

THERE WERE FOUR Coin children.

Nora was ten, bossy but smart.

Then there was John, eight, full of zest and always ready for an adventure.

Third was five-year-old Tom. He was gentle and very loyal.

And finally, there was Madeleine, the toddler. She was eighteen months old.

The children lived with their mother and father in the country in Northern Ireland.

Those are the characters, now the story.

It started on a Sunday, the first one of the summer holidays. As soon as breakfast was over Nora announced, 'We're going to the base.'

They all hurried from their house, out of the gate and up the narrow lane to Mr Richardson's farm. The first part of the lane was lined with copper beech trees and where the trees ended stood a cottage. Mr Richardson owned all the land on either side of the lane but he'd rented the cottage to Danny, a garage mechanic who always smelt of tobacco and petrol.

Danny was sitting outside his house in a deck-chair. He had a long, freckled face, and strange grey eyes.

'Hello bad pennies!' he said, which was how he usually greeted them. 'All well today?'

'Fine,' said Nora abruptly.

Danny was not their favourite person. Last Hallowe'en when they were out trick-or-treating, he had jumped out on them wearing a big white sheet. They'd been terrified.

'Where are you going today, kids?' he said.

'Richardson's,' said Nora.

The children peered through the cottage door behind Danny. The usual bare kitchen looked different. Gone were the old car seats and broken furniture. Instead, Nora could see a dishwasher, a fridge and a washing machine as well as a stereo system, television and video recorder.

'Did you win the lottery?' she asked Danny.

'Nah, didn't win. Just thought it was time I got some new things.'

Nora felt John and Tom slipping their hands into hers. They didn't like talking to Danny, they wanted to get to the base.

'Bye,' said Nora, 'must be off,' and they hurried away up the lane that led to the Richardson's farm. They headed straight for their base.

The base was a den the children had made themselves and they spent all their spare time there. They'd built it behind the empty silage tank in the Richardson's farmyard. The walls were made out of tyres and there were two shed doors for a roof.

'We're at school now, boys,' said Nora in her teacher voice, 'coats on hooks, lunch boxes away, class starts in sixty seconds.'

'Yes, Miss,' chorused John and Tom. They liked the school game, especially when they took turns to be the teacher.

But class had hardly started when Mr Richardson's wife appeared.

'Break time, children.'

'Oh, yes,' they all shouted, except for Madeleine who giggled as Mrs Richardson tickled her under the chin.

Mrs Richardson's kitchen was a square room with an Aga cooker, beside which Granny Richardson sat dozing. Beakers of lemonade and a plate of chocolate biscuits were handed round.

But as they sat there munching in silence, the wail of an approaching siren grew closer and louder.

Granny Richardson stirred and opened her eyes wide. 'What's that?' she asked.

The children ran to the door, just in time to see a fire engine flash by. They could see a column of black smoke rising above the distant copper beeches. It could only be coming from one place.

'Danny's cottage is on fire!' they shouted to Mrs Richardson. 'Can we go and have a look?'

'Don't even think about it!' warned Mrs

Richardson. 'It's too dangerous.'

Reluctantly, the children returned to their base. For the first time ever, they didn't want to be there. They wanted to see the fire.

Quietly they watched Mrs Richardson through a crack in the wall of the base. When she finally left the room, they decided to sneak out and discover what was going on at the cottage.

'Right, now's our chance,' said Nora, picking up Madeleine.

One by one they left the base and sprinted across the fields to Danny's cottage. And there they saw the most amazing sight. Enormous red tongues of fire were leaping out of the downstairs windows and back in through the windows above. Firemen were running and shouting to each other, and there was a large hose pumping water in through the front door.

Danny stood by one of the fire engines.

'What about my stuff?' he shouted.

'There'll not be much left in there now,' a fireman yelled back. 'You'll be lucky if there's even a house left by this evening.'

As Danny turned away, Nora thought she saw him smile, although through the smoke, she couldn't be sure.

Chapter Two

THE WHOLE EVENING was taken up with talking about the fire. Nora and the boys could think of nothing else. What had started it? Would there be anything left? What would Danny do now?

'I suppose it makes a change from talking about your base all day long,' said Mum, 'but remember, whatever you do, don't go near that burnt out cottage – it's dangerous – burnt out rafters could fall and kill you.'

Mum repeated her warning the next morning as they all piled out of the house.

'OK,' Nora shouted back. 'I'll look after everyone, don't worry.'

They hurried out of their gate, but were halted immediately by an enormous tractor pulling a trailer half-filled with grass. It could only be heading for the silage tank at Mr Richardson's farm. The silage tank where the children had built their base!

'Oh no,' wailed Nora.

'That's the end of our base,' said John gloomily.

They had known all along that once the tank was filled with grass for the animals, their tyres

would be used as weights to hold down the
plastic cover. Then the whole area would be
out of bounds to them.

'It's not fair.' John was close to tears.

'Right,' said Nora. 'No time for tears – there
must be somewhere else we can go. Time to
find a bigger, better base.'

John and Tom looked at her blankly.

'I liked our base,' said Tom.

Madeleine gurgled in agreement.

'Hey! What about Danny's?' said Nora. 'We're
not supposed to go into the cottage but no one
said anything about not going into his yard.'

They rushed through the tunnel of copper beeches to Danny's ruined cottage and stared in amazement. It looked much worse now the firemen had gone. They peered through the scorched hole that was once the front door.

The staircase inside, now as black as charcoal, rose into nothingness – the ceiling and first floor were entirely burnt away. The boys stared in every window while Nora took Madeleine round to look for a new base in the backyard. She found several outbuildings including a ramshackle garden shed. There were holes in the roof, but she knew at once it would suit them fine.

'John,' she bellowed, 'Tom!'

The boys came running.

'Look,' she said, 'our new base.'

They scavenged boards from the compost heap and balanced them on bricks to make shelves. They found a kitchen table and two old chairs in one of the outbuildings and a box of old whiskey bottles which they lined up on the window ledge for decoration. They even made curtains out of some old sheets they found lying around. By evening, it was the most brilliant base ever . . .

Chapter Three

THE NEXT DAY, the Coins couldn't wait to get back to their new base.

'We'll be in Danny's yard, nowhere near the house,' they called to Mum, leaving her no time to argue. But when they reached the base, it looked different.

'Someone's moved the chairs,' said John.

They had.

'And the table.'

That too.

'And someone's been smoking,' sniffed Tom. There were flattened cigarette butts all over the floor.

At that moment they heard a tractor coming up the lane. Nora whipped Madeleine out of the pram, and the four of them hid behind the piggery wall.

The tractor stopped outside Danny's gate.

'Hello!' they heard.

They all stood up. It was Mr Richardson.

'I was just passing when I noticed the pram,' he said.

Mr Richardson was an enormous strapping fellow. 'You weren't in the burnt out house?'

'No,' said Nora.

'Mr Richardson, do you smoke?' John asked.

'I do not,' said Mr Richardson. 'Why do you ask? Are you doing a bit of detective work? Trying to find out how the fire started?'

'No!' said Nora. 'And of course we didn't think it was you. It's just that . . .'

'What?'

'We've made a new base, Mr Richardson. Would you like to see it?'

Mr Richardson whistled when he saw the whiskey bottles. 'You children drink a lot!' he laughed.

That was when they heard Tom shouting from inside the piggery. 'Quick. I've found something.'

Everyone crowded into the small, square, smelly room to have a look.

'Here,' said Tom. He lifted away a tarpaulin. Hidden underneath were half-a-dozen petrol cans and some oily rags.

Mr Richardson whistled again and then rushed out. Nora went after him.

'Can we keep our base?' she called, following him towards the gate where the tractor was parked.

'What?'

He took a mobile phone from the cab.

'Our new base. Can we keep it?'

'Why not.' He began dialling. 'We don't
need it.'

At the other end the phone was answered.

'Police?' said Mr Richardson. 'I think you'd
better come down to Danny O'Hara's cottage.

There's something you should see.'

Before they had a chance to ask any questions, Mum appeared.

'Hmm, very nice,' she said as she inspected the base. 'Just make sure you keep away from that cottage. Now, come on home with me, I've made some scones.'

As they walked home, a police car came down the lane. It stopped alongside and the driver put his head out the window.

'Hello, Mrs Coin. What interesting neighbours you have,' he said.

'Do you mean Danny? Where is he? What happened, then?'

'It seems he filled the house with stereos and fridges and all sorts of stolen goods, took out insurance, and watched the whole lot go up in smoke.'

'Danny, an arsonist?' said Mum.

'I didn't say that.'

They walked on.

'What's an arsonist?' asked Nora.

'Someone who sets fire to buildings.'

'But now he doesn't have anywhere to live,' said Nora. 'It doesn't make sense.'

'It does if he makes money.'

'How?'

'Say he steals a television. Say he gets someone to promise to pay him money if it gets burnt in a fire. Then he starts the fire himself. Then he gets the money.'

'Oh,' said Nora, remembering what she had seen in Danny's kitchen. 'I think I understand.'

Chapter Four

WEDNESDAY WAS MISTY. Nora and John had a plan.

'Mum, can we take your little make-up mirror to the base?'

'What on earth for?'

'For flashing messages,' said Nora quickly.

'But there isn't any sun!'

'It's a game, Mum,' said John.

'All right, but don't break it.'

Nora picked up Madeleine and they all ran out. At Danny's gate, John carefully wedged the mirror into a slit he made in the top of a stick.

Seconds later, they were all hidden in the rhododendron bush behind their base. They could hear someone talking inside.

John wriggled along the ground with the stick and hoisted it up to the window. He had got the idea from one of his Tintin books.

Suddenly, a gust of wind blew, just as he was about to see who was inside, and the mirror tumbled out onto the floor with a clatter.

'What was that?' came a gruff voice.

Three soldiers rushed out of the base. They had boot polish on their faces and they each held a very large gun.

'What the hell do you think you're doing?' shouted the biggest one. He was a Corporal.

'You're in our base,' muttered John.

'You scared the wits out of us,' said a second soldier.

'He didn't mean to.' Nora stepped out of the rhododendron bush with Madeleine. Tom followed.

'Oh no,' said the Corporal. 'One was bad enough, but four children is just too much.'

'If anyone has the right to be frightened, it's my brother,' continued Nora.

Now it was the soldiers' turn to apologise.

'Sorry – we won't harm you,' they said.

'He's only eight.'

'We didn't mean to,' the Corporal said, quietly.

'Grown men frightening a boy.' Nora sensed victory.

'We're very, very sorry,' he continued and the other soldiers nodded in agreement. 'So this is your base. We've been here before, you know.'

'We know.'

'We hide in here and smoke. It's the only place we can come where our Sergeant won't find us.

He's an absolute monster. He's always making us run and crawl and sweat, so we like to come here for a break.'

The Corporal paused and looked at Nora seriously.

'Listen,' he said, 'can I ask you a big favour?'

'A question's always free,' said Nora. She'd got this quip from Dad.

'We've got another week of training. Can we come back here?'

'Depends on my brothers,' said Nora.

'I understand,' said the Corporal. A giant bar of chocolate appeared from his pocket and he slowly started to unwrap it.

'I'm Dave, that's Jason and this is Pete,' he said turning to point at the other two soldiers.

The smell of chocolate hung in the misty air.

'Not a bad base,' said Pete.

'Definitely,' agreed Jason.

'But the roof leaks,' said Nora, quick as a flash. 'Yeah?'

'I could get Dad's toolbox,' said John, 'no trouble.'

'I get it,' said Dave, 'we fix the roof and in return, we can come and hide in here and no one says a word about it to anybody.'

John and Tom nodded.

'Deal!' said Nora.

'Is she allowed chocolate?' asked Corporal Dave, pointing at Madeleine.

'We couldn't eat it and not give her some,' said Nora.

'Or she'd scream,' said John bluntly.

'Me, too,' said Tom.

'Oh dear! Well, we don't want that. We've caused enough trouble already.'

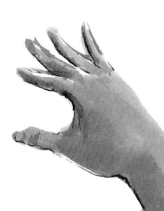

Chapter Five

THAT SAME EVENING, as the four children
made their way happily up the lane towards
home, they heard a rumbling noise.

'It's a dinosaur,' muttered Tom.

But it was only Mr Richardson on his tractor.
He slowed down when he saw the children
and stopped beside them.

'How are you, children?' he asked.

Nora sensed something unpleasant coming.

'Listen, children,' he said. 'Bad news. The
bulldozers are coming Monday to knock down
the rest of Danny's house, so they might as well

do the lot while they're here – the piggery, the outbuildings, and I'm afraid, your base.'

'But why,' wailed John, his eyes filling with tears. 'We've just fixed the roof today, it's perfect.'

'I tell you what,' added the farmer quickly, 'when I have the next load of tyres delivered, you help yourself and build another base on the same site, and I promise it's yours forever.'

The children were not convinced. A whole summer without any base, never mind the best base ever, lay ahead.

Desperate times require desperate measures.
Sitting up in bed that night, Nora clicked on
her torch and wrote a letter:

Dear Dave Jason and Pete,
Our base is going to be bulldozed.
Please help us.
Yours very, very sincerely,
Nora Coin (aged 10)

While Mum and Dad were watching TV, Nora crept into the downstairs room where Tom and John slept. She was going to climb out of the window and bring the letter to the base where the soldiers would be sure to find it.

John sat up in bed.

'What are you doing?' he asked.

'I've written a letter to the soldiers. I'm going to leave it in the base.'

'What's it say?'

'Please help us!'

'I'm coming with you,' said John.

'Me, too,' piped up Tom.

A minute later, they were running up the moonlit lane under the copper beeches.

'What's that?' asked Tom as a noise in the
trees made him jump.

'It's only an owl,' said Nora, trying to be
brave.

'It's spooky,' said Tom.

'Go home, then,' snapped John.

'No way!'

The children slipped through Danny's gates

and ran across the yard. The door of the base was open. Inside, it was as black as a coal hole.

They stopped, half-a-dozen paces short of the door.

'It's a bit scary,' whispered Tom.

'Everything looks different in the dark, that's all,' said Nora, although her heart was beating at twice its usual pace.

Tom held her hand, and she felt John taking the other.

'When I say go, we go in, put the letter on the shelf, come out and run home,' she said.

They moved forward. They reached the doorway. They stepped into darkness.

'Gotcha, you horrible kids!' a voice hissed. It was Danny. He grabbed Nora's wrist. She dropped the letter and screamed.

'The police are after me,' he shouted. 'You're the little sneaks who told them what was in the piggery. You deserve all you get. I'm going to teach you a lesson you'll never forget. You're going to help me burn your house down.'

John lashed out. Tom bit and Nora slipped her thin wrist from Danny's grasp. Half-running, half-stumbling, the children turned and ran across the yard and into the lane.

'I'll get you,' shouted Danny, running after them.

Suddenly, there was a car coming up the lane towards them, its lights flickering through the darkness.

'It's Dad,' shouted Nora.

The children ran along the grass verge towards Dad's car. Dad braked hard. Danny was caught in the headlights. He turned and started to run back up the road. Then, suddenly, there was Mr Richardson's tractor coming the other way.

'Stay where you are, Danny,' they heard Mr Richardson shouting, 'we've got you.'

Danny ran towards the wall but he only managed to get one leg over before Mr Richardson jumped down from the tractor cab and caught him. A few minutes later, the police came, sirens screaming, and took Danny away.

Chapter Six

THE CHILDREN GOT into Dad's car. He explained that Mum had noticed they weren't in their beds and had sent him out to look for them. Then she had phoned the Richardsons who alerted the police.

When they got home they were given cocoa and toast and sent straight to bed. Luckily, Mum seemed more relieved than cross.

That night the children slept soundly – although Nora was certain that sometime in the early morning she heard the roar of a helicopter. A dream of course, she told herself.

Or was it?

The next morning, John – he was always up first – scampered in and shouted, 'Come out to the garden, quickly!'

'What is it?' she said, leaping out of bed.

'Come on,' he shouted.

Nora didn't bother to put on her slippers or her dressing gown. She ran out into the garden in her nightdress, and there, down by the stream, the glorious shape that was their base stood waiting with Nora's letter pinned to the door and signed:

Thank you, from Pete, Dave and Jason

'However did that get there?' said Dad, amazed.

But the Coin children just grinned. It was their secret.

Yellow Bananas are bright, funny, brilliantly imaginative stories written by some of today's top writers. All the books are beautifully illustrated in full colour.

So if you've enjoyed this story, why not pick another from the bunch?

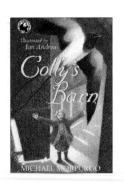

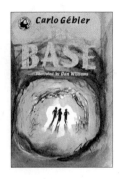

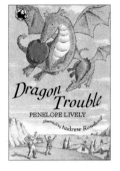